DATE DUE

Demco No. 62-0549

Here are some other Redfeather Books you will enjoy

Alvin's Famous No-Horse
by William Harry Harding

The Curse of the Trouble Dolls
by Dian Curtis Regan

Lavender
by Karen Hesse

Sable
by Karen Hesse

Snakes Are Nothing to Sneeze At
by Gabrielle Charbonnet

Stargone John
by Ellen Kindt McKenzie

Twin Surprises
by Susan Beth Pfeffer

Twin Troubles
by Susan Beth Pfeffer

Available in paperback

Gabrielle Charbonnet

TUTU MUCH BALLET

Illustrated by Abby Carter

A REDFEATHER BOOK

Henry Holt and Company • *New York*

For my husband — G. C.
For Samantha — A. C.

Henry Holt and Company, Inc.
Publishers since 1866
115 West 18th Street
New York, New York 10011

Henry Holt is a registered trademark of Henry Holt and Company, Inc.
Text copyright © 1994 by Gabrielle Charbonnet Varela
Illustrations copyright © 1994 by Abby Carter. All rights reserved.
Published in Canada by Fitzhenry & Whiteside Ltd.,
195 Allstate Parkway, Markham, Ontario L3R 4T8.

Library of Congress Cataloging-in-Publication Data
Charbonnet, Gabrielle. Tutu much ballet / Gabrielle Charbonnet ;
illustrated by Abby Carter.   p.   cm.—(A Redfeather book)
Summary: When her grandmother comes to visit during the summer,
Charlotte thinks she will be allowed to go to gymnastics camp with
her best friend, but her mother and grandmother insist that she take
ballet lessons instead.
[1. Ballet dancing—Fiction.   2. Mothers and daughters—Fiction.
3. Grandmothers—Fiction.   4. Friendship—Fiction.]   I. Carter,
Abby, ill.   II. Title.   III. Series: Redfeather books.
PZ7.C37355Tu   1994   [Fic]—dc20   93-38846

ISBN 0-8050-3063-8
First Edition—1994
Printed in the United States of America on acid-free paper.∞

10   9   8   7   6   5   4   3   2   1

Contents

TUTU MUCH BALLET

1

Day Camp at Last

Charlotte waited by the front door impatiently, looking through the glass. She would have waited outside on the porch, but it was a typical summer day—beastly hot and muggy. It would probably rain later on, as it did almost every day in the summer.

Brandy, her family's golden retriever, sat by her feet, ready to leap into action at the slightest hint of an intruder. Charlotte saw Annabel running up the sidewalk toward Charlotte's house. Her face was red and her long dark braids were flying back like kite tails. Charlotte yanked the door open.

"Hi!" She pulled Annabel in. "That was fast. I called you only five minutes ago."

Annabel nodded, glad to be in the air conditioning.

" 'S only four blocks," she panted. "What's going on? What's the good news?"

"Come on. Upstairs." They ran up to Charlotte's room, and Charlotte shut the door. She sat on her bed, bouncing up and down, a big smile on her face. Annabel couldn't help laughing.

"*What?*" she said.

"My grandmother broke her hand," Charlotte announced gleefully.

Annabel looked at her. "*That's* the good news? Charlotte, how can you be happy about that? She's your gra—"

"Annabel—don't you see? She broke her hand, and now I can't go see her for two weeks. She's coming here, because she needs help doing things. That's what I'm happy about—not her hand. Sheesh." Charlotte rolled her eyes.

"Oh, my gosh—really?" Annabel started bouncing up and down too. "That's fabulous! Now you can go to day camp with me!"

"Right. I'm glad you finally get it."

"Have you asked your mom yet? I can't believe this luck."

Charlotte nodded. "Uh-huh. She said she'd talk to Daddy about it. You know, she made her face—" Charlotte imitated it, and Annabel snickered. "—but they can't say no. Nana's coming tonight, and I bet tomorrow we'll go pick up the forms and register me."

Charlotte was totally psyched. For the first time ever, she and Annabel would be taking the bus to day camp together every morning. They would meet on the corner, both with their backpacks full of swimsuits and towels and lunches. They would do gymnastics together, and eat lunch together, and swim together and everything.

"Yay!" Annabel cheered. "This is going to be the best summer ever!" They slapped high fives, then low fives, then fives on the side.

They played with Charlotte's pet iguana, Spike, in Charlotte's room for a while. Charlotte had just bought a new little harness for Spike to wear outside, and they tried it on him. Then Annabel called home and asked if she could have lunch at Charlotte's house. Of course her mom said yes.

So Mrs. Hastings fixed them both peanut-butter sandwiches.

"Gee, this is great," Annabel said, peering at her sandwich. "You're lucky—my mom never makes me and Michael lunch on the weekends. We have to get it ourselves."

"Really?" Charlotte chewed thoughtfully. She supposed she could make her own lunch if she had to. "What do you make?"

"Well, a sandwich, like this. Only I usually leave the crusts on. And we have brown bread at my house."

Charlotte wrinkled her nose. "I'm not crazy about whole-wheat bread, myself."

"I'm used to it. Mom says she likes a bread that can fight back. Sometimes for lunch we used to stick hot dogs on a barbecue fork and hold them over a stove burner."

"Really? Geez. I'm only allowed to use the microwave." Roasting a hot dog over an open burner seemed so daring, somehow. Charlotte wondered if she could ever try it. Maybe if her parents and Susan, their housekeeper, were all out of the house at the same time.

"Yeah. But since Mom found us letting the hot dogs catch on fire just to see what happened, she makes us boil or microwave them instead."

Later Annabel went home to dinner. "Call me and tell me what happens," she said, waving her hand to show that her fingers were crossed. Charlotte had to go to the airport that night to meet her grandmother.

"I will," Charlotte called back.

Charlotte was surprised by how much older Nana looked when they picked her up. She had seen her only six months ago, at Christmas. Now Nana looked more tired, and maybe her hair was grayer. On her left wrist was a metal-and-canvas brace.

"You wouldn't believe how helpless this darn thing makes me feel," Nana said as they were driving home. "It really irks me not to be able to weed my own flower bed and make my own meals. Of course, the girls at church have been very thoughtful, very thoughtful indeed. . . ."

In the backseat, Charlotte smiled to herself.

Sometimes Nana cracked her up. "Darn" and "irks." And Charlotte knew the "girls" at church were probably as old as Nana—almost seventy. Annabel's grandmother had visited the Bentleys at Easter, but she was pretty different from Nana. Jazzier, somehow. She had taken Annabel and Michael to the racetrack.

"Charlotte, honey, I'm speaking to you."

"Oh, sorry, Nana, I didn't hear you."

"I said, tell me about your plans for the summer, dear."

Charlotte launched into an enthusiastic recital about how she and Annabel had planned the whole summer: day camp, letting Spike and Annabel's green snake, Wilfred, play together, hanging out at the mall . . .

"Hmm," Nana said. "I'm sure if we put our heads together, dear, we'll be able to think up a few more challenging activities for you as well. Henry, dear, please slow down. We're not racing that Volvo next to us, are we?" she cautioned Charlotte's father.

Charlotte raised her eyebrows. Challenging activities? In the summer? What did Nana mean?

"Now, Aileen, are you still working in that doctor's office?" Nana asked Charlotte's mother. Mrs. Hastings worked part time doing computer work for a radiology clinic.

"Yes, of course, Mother. I enjoy it. We got in a lovely new program last week, and I've been setting it up."

"Goodness, all these modern computer things! I simply don't understand them—never will. I was always thankful that I could devote myself full time to my family." She turned around in her seat and smiled at Charlotte and Mrs. Hastings.

Charlotte looked over at her mother. Mrs. Hastings had a frozen smile on her face. Charlotte wondered if her mother was going to enjoy Nana's visit. Well, at least Charlotte knew *she* would— Nana's being here meant that she was going to day camp with Annabel.

2

Much Too Pretty for That

"What!" Charlotte cried, staring at her mother.

It was two days after they had picked up Nana at the airport, and Charlotte, Nana, and Mrs. Hastings were in the breakfast room.

"Now, Charlotte," Mrs. Hastings said calmly, "let's just think about it."

"I don't want to think about it. I already *know* I don't want to go to ballet school. I want to go to day camp and take gymnastics with Annabel. Why can't I?"

"Now, dear, listen to your mother," Charlotte's grandmother said. "You don't want to be all rough-and-tumble in a gym class." She smiled affectionately at Charlotte. "You're much too pretty for that. Ballet will be so much nicer for you. I loved ballet class when I was your age, and your mother did too. Didn't you, dear?" she asked Charlotte's mother.

"It's true. And Charlotte, you'll get to wear all sorts of pretty costumes, and listen to wonderful music. I know you'll enjoy it."

Charlotte was practically in tears. She couldn't believe it. All of her and Annabel's plans were being wrecked. Not only were they not going to let her go to day camp, but they were going to sign her up for *ballet*, which she knew she would hate.

"Mom. Nana," she began, trying not to cry. "I know other kids like ballet. But I really don't want to do it. I had my heart set on gymnastics class with Annabel. And they do other things too, like swim, and take art classes. . . ." Maybe the art classes would satisfy them, she hoped. "I don't *want* to do ballet. It's sissy. I won't like it." Her lower lip was trembling and she bit it to keep it still. On the other hand, if she cried, they might change their minds. She let it tremble.

"Dear," her grandmother said sternly, "sissy is

not the word I would use to describe such a beautiful art form as ballet. And if you think learning poise, grace, and coordination is a sissy pursuit, then all I can say is perhaps you need a little bit more sissiness in your life. When I heard that your mother had allowed you to get a *reptile* for a pet, why, I . . ." She broke off, seeming unable to put her feelings about Charlotte's iguana into words.

Charlotte looked at her mother, her eyes wide. Mrs. Hastings pursed her lips.

"What's wrong with Spike?" Charlotte said. "He's beautiful! I love him—he's mine." She had gotten him for her last birthday—after she had convinced her mother to take back the fashion-doll dream house her mother had thought she would like.

"And that name—Spike," Nana said. "It's so ugly. It's like naming him 'Thug' or something. My goodness, when I was your age . . ."

"But you're *not* my age! I hate ballet and I love Spike, and nothing is going to change that!" Charlotte yelled.

Her mother and grandmother looked at her, shocked. Charlotte had never yelled at her mom before, and certainly not at her grandmother. She knew she was in big trouble now. She thought about Annabel, at home waiting for her to call so they could plan their first day at day camp together. The whole summer was ruined. She burst into tears and ran upstairs to her room.

On Wednesday afternoon after work, Charlotte's mother took her shopping at the mall. They went to a special dance store, and Mrs. Hastings picked out three sleeveless black leotards, three pairs of pale pink tights, and some very cute black ballet slippers. The ballet school had sent them a list of what to buy.

Charlotte looked at them glumly. She always loved getting new things, and if these had been for gymnastics class, she would have been thrilled. But it was hard to be excited when the leotards were only symbols of what she was being forced to do.

"And look, sweetheart—aren't these little hair

things darling? What are they called? Everyone's wearing them."

Charlotte looked at the pile of fabric-covered hair elastics. "Scrunchies," she said.

"Well, I know you have to wear your hair up off your neck, so let's get some. They look fun." Mrs. Hastings smiled at Charlotte cheerfully.

"Okay," Charlotte said with a sigh. She picked out a black one, a striped pink one, and then a neat one with fluorescent colors dribbled all over it. It would look great with jeans.

"Oh, honey, are you sure you want that one?" Charlotte's mother said.

"Sure. What's wrong with it?"

"Well, it's not very attractive, is it?"

"Just because it's not pretty doesn't mean it isn't neat. I like this one," Charlotte said firmly.

"Oh well, okay, honey."

Charlotte rolled her eyes as she walked behind her mother to the cash register. Her mom still wanted her to dress like a little girl—or even worse, like *her* when she was a little girl. Her mom really had to get with it. This was the nineties.

Mrs. Hastings paid for the clothes and they left the store. "I love shopping, don't you?" she asked. "It can be exhausting sometimes, but it's fun to look in all the different stores. Let's go in here—they have some adorable outfits."

Charlotte followed her mother into a clothing store. She thought the clothes in here were stuffy, especially the kids' things. They looked as if they were for ten-year-old bankers. Charlotte trailed her mother around for a while, but she couldn't work up any interest.

"Let's go to the pet store, Mom. Maybe they have something new for Spike."

They went to Petworld, where Charlotte had first picked out Spike. Inside, she immediately headed for the reptile section.

"Look! A new iguana book." Charlotte flipped through the pages to see if there was anything she didn't already know. In the back it had a comprehensive diet plan, with a chart of different protein sources and vegetables that iguanas like. It was similar to something Charlotte already had, but more detailed. And it listed places where she could order Spike's vitamins, Reptovite brand, through the mail. Sometimes they were difficult to find.

"I'll take it," she told the woman behind the counter, pulling her allowance out of her wallet. Charlotte's mother didn't say anything. Charlotte knew that when her mom had been little, she had had pet rabbits. Rabbits seemed so boring to Charlotte—like cute, living bath mats.

3

Not Cut Out
to Be a Ballerina

That night after dinner, Mrs. Hastings knocked on Charlotte's bedroom door.

"Come in," Charlotte said.

Her mother hesitated, then sat down next to Charlotte on the bed. She put her arm around Charlotte's shoulders and stroked the blond curls off her face.

"Darling," she began. "I know you don't feel very happy about ballet class right now. If I weren't so sure that you'll love it, I wouldn't make you try it. But I know once you're there, you're going to have a wonderful time. When I was a little girl, I couldn't wait for ballet class. I would practice every day in front of my mirror at home."

Charlotte remained quiet. She had seen pictures of her mother as a little girl, in various ballet costumes for recitals.

"You know why I think you'll enjoy ballet?"

"Because I'll be learning poise and grace and coordination?" Charlotte said automatically.

Her mother laughed. "No, that's not why—no matter what Nana says. No, I think you'll like ballet because you're so much like me. From the time you were very, very small, you've done things that I did when I was little. You like the same books, and enjoy the same games, and other things. Well . . ." She hesitated. "Except for Spike, of course."

Charlotte gave a small smile. She couldn't imagine her mother playing with an iguana, or kissing it, the way she did Spikey.

"All the same, Mom, I have a feeling I'm not going to like ballet."

"Well, darling, please just give it a try."

"Like I have a choice," Charlotte said.

The following Sunday, Charlotte and Annabel were sitting in the double swing on Annabel's front porch.

"So, you start tomorrow, huh?" Annabel asked. She still felt kind of mad at Charlotte's mother about the ballet business. Since they had found out, they had played at Annabel's house almost all the time—not at Charlotte's. Annabel said she just couldn't face Mrs. Hastings yet.

"Yep," Charlotte said glumly.

"Well, let's look on the bright side," Annabel said. "Your ballet class lasts only five weeks. It could be worse—day camp lasts for six. Or you *could* have been signed up for all summer long."

"That's true," Charlotte said, and sighed. She knew Annabel was trying to cheer her up.

"And your leotards and tights are pretty—we just wear shorts and T-shirts to camp. It'll be nice to look like a real ballerina." Privately, Annabel thought that she herself would prefer *not* to look like a real ballerina, but of course she didn't tell Charlotte that.

"Uh-huh," Charlotte said.

"Maybe you'll like it after all," Annabel said desperately.

Charlotte turned and looked at her.

"Well, remember—you didn't think you liked

snakes, either. But then you did." It had taken Charlotte a while to recognize Wilfred's charm. Both girls smiled at the memory.

"You think I'll start to like ballet when I get used to it?" Charlotte asked doubtfully. She tried to imagine herself moving gracefully in front of a big mirror.

"Well, yeah. It's possible."

"Hmmm," Charlotte said.

On the first morning of ballet class, Charlotte rode silently in the car, next to her mother. Trying not to cry, she clutched her little tote of leotards and tights. She felt scared and nervous about going to a new place full of strangers, and wished that Annabel were with her. What if she was absolutely terrible? What if she was a total klutz? What if everyone laughed at her? Charlotte leaned her head against the car window and swallowed a big lump in her throat. This was the worst idea her mother had ever had.

The sign on the building said "Gray's Ballet Academy." They went in, and Mrs. Hastings helped Charlotte find the classroom. At the door,

Mrs. Hastings kissed Charlotte and smiled at her. "Now remember, darling, I'll be back at noon to pick you up. I thought we'd go have lunch out today, as a special treat. We could go to Camellia Grill. Would you like that?"

Charlotte nodded.

"Do you want me to come in and meet your teacher?"

"No, thanks. I'll just go in." Two girls around Charlotte's age passed them and went into the class. One of them went to Charlotte's school. Charlotte liked her okay.

"All right, then. Bye, honey."

"Bye, Mom."

"So? Tell me all," Annabel commanded later that afternoon. Charlotte had called her as soon as Annabel had gotten home from day camp. "No, wait—I'll come over."

At Charlotte's house they went upstairs. Annabel went over to Spike's aquarium. "Hey, Spikums. How's my nephew? You're a big boy. Yes, you are." Spike rotated one eye to look at her. He toddled forward on his strong little legs and

came closer to the glass. He had a bit of a spinach leaf hanging from his mouth.

"Say hello to Aunt Annabel, Spike," Charlotte said, smiling. They joked about being aunts to each other's pets.

"Okay, now tell me how it went, " Annabel said, sitting on Charlotte's bed. "What did you do? Are the other kids nice? Are they all girls?"

"No, there're two boys, too. One of them is the son of the owner. Most of the other kids seem all right, but some of them have been doing this longer and are pretty good at it. Cathy Soames is in my class."

"Oh? She's nice."

"Uh-huh. But Louisa Ridley's in my class too."

"Louisa the Please-a? Yuck. That goody-goody."

"Yeah. You know, it's not like I hate ballet or anything—I like watching the *Nutcracker* on television at Christmas."

Annabel nodded.

"It's just that I don't want to *be* a ballet dancer. My mom is acting like I have to do everything she did when she was little—be exactly like her. And I don't want to." Charlotte paused. "When I tried to tell her how I felt, she just looked disappointed, like I wasn't her daughter or something. It was awful."

Annabel couldn't think of anything to say. She thought Mrs. Hastings was weird. At least weird about this.

"What exactly was class like?" she asked.

Charlotte sighed. "Well, first we all changed in a small room off the main one. We each have a locker, and there are little benches."

Annabel nodded. "Like the locker room at school."

"Yeah. But nicer, and pinker. The boys changed somewhere else—the broom closet or something. Then in the big room we did warmup exercises, like stretching and breathing. I didn't feel too stupid because everyone was doing it." Charlotte got up and went to adjust the clip-on lamp over Spike's aquarium.

"In the big room," she continued, "one whole wall is mirrors from floor to ceiling. There's a wooden barre in front of the mirrors, and sometimes we have to hang on to it. Then we did some really boring exercises, practicing the five basic positions of ballet."

She showed Annabel the five basic positions. Some of them she couldn't do perfectly yet.

"Just five positions?" Annabel frowned. She thought ballet looked a lot more complicated than that.

"Uh-huh. Five for the feet and five for the arms. We did those forever, then we practiced leaping a little bit. At the end of class we sat on the floor and watched a short movie about ballet."

"Did you like any of it?" Annabel asked.

"I liked the leaping part. The other stuff and the movie were pretty dull," Charlotte said. "I would give anything just to wear shorts and to go to day camp and run around and swim."

Annabel nodded seriously. "You know, Charlotte," she said, "I remember when I was just starting gymnastics. They made us do baby stuff, like cartwheels and somersaults, just to get us used to it. You'll probably start more interesting stuff soon."

Charlotte looked at Annabel. "Annabel. I'm not

cut out to be a ballerina. I don't care if we move on to more interesting stuff. It isn't interesting to *me*. Don't you start on me too," she said crossly.

"Sorry, sorry."

4

An Ally!

The next morning Charlotte's mother drove her to ballet class. Charlotte had a fresh leotard and tights in her tote. Oh well, she thought. Here we go again. Suddenly Charlotte wished she would become really sick so she could stay home. She concentrated on her throat to see if it was sore. It wasn't. She felt her forehead for a temperature. It was cool.

The thought of facing all those strangers again did make her feel sick to her stomach, though. In ballet, it seemed as if everyone watched you all the time.

When Mrs. Hastings tried to kiss her good-bye, Charlotte wouldn't kiss her back. "Bye," she said, getting out of the car unenthusiastically.

"Have a good class, sweetie. I'll pick you up at noon."

Charlotte nodded without looking back, then walked slowly toward the building. She glanced around at the outside of the building. Maybe she could just hide somewhere instead of going to class. But out of the corner of her eye, she saw her mother's car still waiting by the curb. Charlotte sighed and went in.

In the changing room she started to get into her leotard. Several other girls were changing too. They all smiled at one another. Charlotte tried to smile back.

Cathy Soames had the locker next to hers. "Hi," she said.

"Hi." Charlotte tried not to look too miserable. She knew it was a drag being around a complainer.

Cathy got into her black leotard and pink tights quickly. She gave Charlotte a little smile. "Every summer I want to go to horse camp. Every summer I go to ballet school. When I'm eighteen, I'm going to move away and buy my own horse." She shut her locker and ran out to the big room.

Her mouth open, Charlotte watched Cathy leave. She had an ally! She closed her locker and followed Cathy.

Class that day didn't seem to go as well as the first day. Despite being happy about Cathy Soames, Charlotte felt so tense that it was hard for her to concentrate. When she didn't concentrate, she got out of the rhythm and lost count.

They learned to do several new motions that day: pliés, glissades, and even a beginning arabesque. But several times Charlotte looked up and saw that the entire class was doing something one way, and she was doing it another way all by herself.

The names of the movements were pretty, and when Madame Fisher, the teacher, performed them, they looked elegant and graceful. When Charlotte watched herself in the mirror, she thought she looked short and dumpy, and not very elegant or graceful at all. Maybe ballet was meant for tall people.

Madame Fisher had to correct her posture and positions several times. Even though she did it kindly, Charlotte was embarrassed. And once she started messing up, she couldn't get back on track. When Mrs. Hastings came to pick her up at noon, Charlotte was close to tears.

Her mother saw Charlotte's face and trembling lip. In the car, she smiled gently at Charlotte and patted her knee. Charlotte didn't say anything, but her mother seemed to know she had had a bad day. "It'll go better tomorrow, honey," she said soothingly.

At the thought of having to go back to ballet class the next day, Charlotte's stomach clenched. She would have to face all those kids who had seen her be such a klutz today.

"What are you going to do?" Annabel asked later that afternoon. Annabel's father had set up the hammock in her backyard, and she and Charlotte were lying in it, eating Popsicles.

"I don't know," Charlotte said miserably. "When I think about class, I just want to die." She pushed one foot against the grass to swing them gently.

Annabel licked her Popsicle. "Oh, dang," she muttered when she noticed grape juice dripping onto

her T-shirt. She looked up at Charlotte. "Well, you can't go on like this," she said. "You're going to have an ulcer before the end of the course."

Charlotte nodded. "I don't know what I'm going to do, but I've got to come up with something," she said. "Oh, let's not talk about it. I'm sick of it. What did you do today?"

"We were doing the trampoline." Annabel's face lit up. "I love the trampoline—it's so fun. I like jumping as high as I can." She sucked on her Popsicle for a minute. "Some kids are really good on it—they can do all kinds of stuff. I can do a few things, but not everything. I really want to do a backflip, but I just can't seem to get it. I don't *bend* in the right way." She licked her Popsicle thoughtfully.

"Hmm." Charlotte was a little relieved to hear that there was something Annabel couldn't do perfectly. Sometimes she seemed so *capable* that it was kind of disheartening. "Well, keep trying. I'm sure you'll get it soon."

"I *have* to get it pretty soon. In another week we'll start rehearsing our big show. I'll be in it for

the first time this year. My group will do a floor
routine together, then separate routines on whatever our specialty is."

"That sounds great," Charlotte said enviously.
"So what's the problem?" It sounded exactly like
what she wanted to be doing herself, instead of all
the dainty, repetitive movements in ballet class.

"The problem is that if I can't learn to do a
backflip, the only solo I can do would be the
horse—it doesn't require a backflip. And the
horse is my least favorite thing! It's boring." Annabel finished her Popsicle and started breaking
the stick into little pieces.

Just then Annabel's brother, Michael, leaned
out the kitchen door. "Charlotte, your mom called.
You have to go home for dinner."

Charlotte sighed and rolled out of the hammock. "Oh—I nearly forgot. Mom said I could ask
you to sleep over on Friday. We could rent a
movie. You want to?"

"Sure—that'd be great. She's feeling guilty,
huh?"

"Yep."

*   *   *

That night Charlotte, her parents, and Nana were all sitting around the dinner table. Charlotte played with her fork while she waited for her mother to finish passing the serving dishes.

After she helped herself to some shrimp curry and rice, she had to wait until everyone had everything they wanted. She thought about eating dinner at Annabel's house. Annabel's parents made her and Michael sit with them at the table, and they couldn't watch TV or anything, but it was more casual.

When Charlotte ate there, Annabel just gave her a plate and they all lined up in the kitchen, where Annabel's mom or dad dished out whatever they were eating. No serving bowls. And Annabel and Michael took turns setting the table and clearing it away. They hated doing this and always tried to get out of it. Charlotte thought the idea of having an actual chore sounded grown up.

"So, darling, tell me about class today," Nana said to Charlotte.

"I messed up a bunch of times. Please pass the salt," Charlotte said.

Mrs. Hastings handed her the saltshaker. "Do the other children seem friendly?" she asked.

Charlotte nodded, chewing. "There's a girl in my class that I know from school. Cathy Soames. She seems nice."

"Oh good." Charlotte's mother smiled.

"She doesn't want to be there either. She'd rather go to horse camp."

Mrs. Hastings's eyes narrowed a little.

"Oh, sweetheart," Nana said to Charlotte's mother, "I happened to notice your housekeeper today, passing a damp mop over the wooden floors in the living room!" She laughed, shaking her head. "You'll have to have a little talk with her, I'm afraid. Remember, a well-managed household is a joy to be in." She gave Charlotte's father a meaningful look.

"The floors are sealed with polyurethane, Mother. A damp mop won't hurt them. But thanks anyway." Mrs. Hastings broke off a piece of bread.

"Oh, I see." Nana took a delicate bite of salad. "Charlotte, I haven't told you how much I like the color you chose for your room. That pale yellow is very attractive, and so cheerful." She smiled at

Charlotte across the table. "And your father is very clever to have built those nice shelves to keep everything tidy."

Charlotte's father looked up absentmindedly and managed a vague smile.

"Thank you," Charlotte said.

"Paste wax!" Nana suddenly said.

"What, Mother?" Mrs. Hastings asked.

"Paste wax. I was trying to think of what we always used on our floors to keep them nice. It was paste wax. We would wax the floors and buff them three times before a party, I remember. Oh, they used to shine! Your father always said he could see his reflection in my floors." Nana closed her eyes, thinking back. "I remember one party we gave—this is before you were born, Aileen—I think it was New Year's Eve. I wore a lovely black-and-white gown, and your father was so handsome in his tuxedo. It was after the war, and we had gotten hold of real butter for the pastry shells. . . ."

Charlotte finished her dinner, listening to the story Nana was telling. She loved hearing about when Nana was young, and her grandfather was alive, and her mother was a little girl. It sounded as though Nana had always lived in fancy houses and had thrown fancy parties. Her own mother didn't throw many fancy parties. Sometimes it amazed Charlotte that her mother and Nana were related at all, but other times they seemed just alike.

5

Total Klutz-a-mondo

That Friday, Charlotte was spending the night at Annabel's. They had decided it would be more fun at the Bentleys', because Nana didn't really like them to make noise at Charlotte's house.

After dinner they loaded the dishwasher, then fixed themselves glasses of chocolate milk. Annabel's mother came into the kitchen.

"That was a great dinner, Mrs. Bentley," Charlotte said.

Mrs. Bentley looked surprised. "It was just meat loaf. But I'm glad you liked it, honey. Look, Annabel," she said, holding up a scrap of paper. "I found this cookie recipe in a magazine. It looks pretty simple, and I think we even have all the ingredients. Do you guys want to try making some? I could use a sugar fix."

"Yeah! Thanks, Mom," Annabel said.

Charlotte and Annabel hunted up all the ingredients they would need. Annabel lugged over the big glass container that held the flour.

"So let me tell you about my humiliating day," she said, setting it on the counter.

"Oh no. What happened?" Charlotte asked. She was cutting a stick of butter into little pieces.

"It was pretty bad. Bill, our teacher, wanted us to run through all our trampoline skills." Annabel pulled the brown sugar out of the cupboard and found some vanilla extract. "First Kevin went. He's pretty good. He did a forward somersault, then a jump where he touched his toes out to the side. Then he bent in the middle and touched his toes together out at the front."

"Do y'all have any eggs?" Charlotte asked, looking inside the refrigerator.

"In the door."

"Got it. Okay, what else did he do?"

"Well, he did a funny trick where he bounced a

couple of times, then turned sideways in midair with his hand under his head. He looked like he was lying down in midair. We all laughed. Then he did a perfect backflip."

"Oh," Charlotte said, looking at Annabel. "So who else did backflips?"

"Dustin, Lily, Blake, and Sarah. Not all of them did everything perfectly, and Blake messed up his backflip and had to try it two more times. He finally got it, though, even if his landing did stink."

Charlotte sprayed Pam all over two cookie sheets. Annabel stirred the stiff cookie dough fiercely as she talked. Charlotte hoped she wouldn't spill any of it. "Did we put the salt in?" she asked.

"Yeah. It's always so weird to put salt in cookies."

"Uh-huh. Then what happened?"

"Then it was my turn. The forward somersault was easy. So was the split in midair where I touch my toes. I'm good at that, better than the boys."

"Uh-huh," Charlotte said. Annabel stopped stirring, and they took turns spooning out the batter and dropping it in lumps on the cookie sheets.

"Then I had to do the backflip. I bounced high, as high as I could. It looked so easy when everyone else did it. Then I pulled my knees up and tried to sort of *throw* my body backward." Annabel lifted one knee as she dropped cookies onto the cookie sheet, trying to demonstrate.

"Uh-huh," Charlotte said, licking her spoon.

"And—I don't know what happened. I don't know why I didn't flip backward. But I just fell, fell onto the trampoline on my side."

Charlotte nodded seriously.

"Bill made me try twice more, but I just couldn't do it. The only time I can do it is when he's on the trampoline and helps me flip. Other than that, I'm a total failure."

"No, you're not. You're great at everything else. I bet you're not the only one who couldn't do the backflip. Wasn't there anyone else?"

Annabel shoved the cookie sheets into the oven. They had already turned it on. "Yeah. A kid named Carver. He's the biggest dork in the world."

Charlotte looked at the ground. "Oh."

"We are talking total klutz-a-mondo here, Char."

On Monday Charlotte and Cathy Soames made sure to stand next to each other in class. As they were changing that morning, they realized they lived only four blocks apart.

"Maybe we can take the bus home together," Cathy suggested.

"I'll ask my mom tonight," Charlotte said.

She had a slightly easier time in ballet class that day. She knew everyone's name now, which helped. It still seemed boring most of the time, but she did enjoy the leaping, and they were doing more of that.

Usually for the last half hour of class Madame Fisher gave a little lecture, or showed slides or a short film. Today when the group gathered on the floor at her feet, she pulled down a large diagram of the human body.

"Today we're going to become more familiar with how our bodies work," she told the class, smiling and moving gracefully to one side to get her pointer. She always walked in a smooth, feet-out dancer's walk. Some of the girls in Charlotte's class walked that way too, at least in class. Charlotte wondered if Madame Fisher walked that way even at the grocery store, or when she was cleaning her house.

"This is a diagram of our muscles," Madame Fisher said, pointing at one picture. "And this is our skeletal structure." She pointed to a drawing of a skeleton. The muscle diagram looked like a man with no skin—just pink, ropy muscles covering everything. His behind muscles looked really big.

"Now, we dancers must have an understanding of how our bodies work. This will help us move properly, so that we can perform the most strenuous dance movements without injuring ourselves or causing lasting damage to our bones or muscles. Many a dancer has been forced to retire because she did not learn how her body functioned." She looked out at her class sternly, as if suspecting that this might happen to some of them.

"You are still children, still growing," Madame Fisher said. "Your muscles are not as big and

strong as an adult's. Therefore you must take more care not to develop bad habits that will hurt you later on."

After the lecture Madame Fisher had the class move in different ways to learn how their muscles were pulling and stretching and working together. Charlotte tried to copy her movements exactly, feeling how her bones fit together and how the joints bent in some ways and not in others. It was the most interesting class they had had yet.

At noon Charlotte's mother came to pick her up. Nana was in the car too.

"How was class, dear?" Nana asked.

"Okay. Madame Fisher showed us how our muscles and bones work. It was neat."

"Did you perform any pretty little dances?"

"Uh, no. Not yet. We're still learning the basics."

"Honey, I have to stop at the grocery. We need some almonds to go with the chicken for dinner," Charlotte's mother said. "Then I have to get back to work."

"Okay," Charlotte said.

"I've found," Nana said conspiratorially, "that if I plan my menus a week in advance, and then make a careful list of all the ingredients, I don't have to make any inconvenient emergency runs to the store." She smiled and nodded at Charlotte in the backseat.

Charlotte wondered if she was supposed to remember this for when she was a grown-up.

"Mother, stopping for almonds once in a while isn't really a big deal," Charlotte's mother said. "I still somehow manage to get dinner together every night, don't I, Char?"

"Sure," Charlotte agreed. She saw that her mother's hands were gripping the steering wheel so tightly that the knuckles were white. Nana turned to face forward again, and Charlotte smothered a smile. Maybe her mom was seeing how Charlotte felt sometimes.

6

The Worst Thing

At noon the next day Charlotte and Cathy walked to the bus stop together. It was a hot day with no breeze, and Charlotte was glad the bus stop had a big oak tree shading it.

"Well, twelve days down, thirteen more to go," Cathy said, putting her tote at her feet.

"Ugh, don't remind me," Charlotte moaned, getting out her bus money. The night before, she had asked her parents if she could ride the bus with Cathy. Her mother had looked doubtful, and asked whether Charlotte wouldn't rather that she just pick her up.

"But Mom, you have to leave work every day to do it. Cathy lives only four blocks away, and she takes the bus all the time. It's in a straight line—there's no way I can get lost. All the kids do it."

"Well . . ."

"It seems like it would be all right, Aileen," Charlotte's father said from where he was washing lettuce at the sink. "She's plenty old enough to take the bus home."

Charlotte gave her father a grateful look. Good old Dad.

"My goodness," Nana said, walking into the room. "I hope you're not seriously considering it, dear. Heaven knows it was perfectly all right to take public transportation when you were a child, but nowadays. . . ."

"Mother, what could happen? It's broad daylight, it *is* in a straight line, and she would get off two blocks from our house. And it has been a bit inconvenient for me to leave work every day." She turned to face Charlotte. "Yes, you may take the bus home with Cathy Soames tomorrow after class," she said firmly.

"Oh, thanks, Mom! Thanks, Dad." Charlotte gave them each a big smile. She noticed that Nana looked grumpy, but she knew her mom's decision was final. As she skipped out of the room she heard her mother saying, "Of course it's all right, Mother. It will be fine. Goodness, she's ten years old, almost eleven."

Now she and Cathy were waiting at the stop. The bus came, and they got on. They found two seats together at the back.

"Yep," Cathy continued. "Thirteen more days till the big end-of-class recital."

Charlotte smiled at her. "What do you mean? What kind of recital?"

Cathy dug around in her tote and found some banana taffy. She offered some to Charlotte.

"You know, our class's recital. We have to give a little show for our parents and the students in other classes. We do it every year. With costumes and all."

The banana taffy seemed to choke Charlotte. "What?" she gasped.

Cathy looked at her. "You didn't know? No one told you?"

"No! I don't believe it. What kind of show are

you talking about? Does everyone have to be in it, or are you picked? When is it?"

"Well, last year we did a scene from the *Nut-cracker*. I was a dancing sugarplum. I think this year we're going to do a scene from *Swan Lake*. I guess we'll all be swans. Louisa Ridley will probably be the lead swan."

Charlotte couldn't get over it. No one had told her. She wondered if her mother knew, and had hidden it from her. There was one thing that was completely, perfectly, totally, utterly definite: there was no way she was going to be in that recital. No way, no how.

"Oh, but of course you'll be in it, dear!" Nana exclaimed. "I imagine that Madame Fisher will choose a scene that will let all of your little classmates participate. It's *Swan Lake,* is it?" She looked excited. "What a lovely ballet! What day is the performance?"

"The last day of class," Charlotte snarled.

Nana checked the kitchen calendar. "Perfect! I'm scheduled to leave the very next day. Oh, I wouldn't miss your first recital for the world, darling. Wait until I tell all my friends. I'll have to get new film for my camera. . . ."

Charlotte stared at her in horror. "Nana, you don't understand. I can't be in that recital. I can't dance in front of anyone. It would be a total nightmare."

Nana paused in making their sandwiches for lunch. Her hand was better, and she didn't have to wear her brace all the time. "But why, dear? Don't you want to show off what you've learned?"

"All I've learned is that I'm the world's biggest klutz at ballet," Charlotte said desperately. "Mom can't make me be in that show. She just can't."

Nana cut their sandwiches into quarters and arranged them neatly on plates. Then she put the plates on the kitchen table, sat down, and unfolded her napkin. "Come, sit down and eat, dear. Let's talk about it."

Charlotte sat down heavily and looked at her sandwich. "I can't eat. I'll be sick," she said sadly.

"It's funny you should say that. Sometimes I've felt ill when I was very nervous. Sick to my stomach," Nana said, then took a small bite of her sandwich.

Charlotte looked at her grandmother with interest. Grown-ups didn't talk about things like this very often—feeling nervous and petrified. They sort of plodded forward no matter what. "Really?"

"Yes. Your saying that brought back a memory from a long time ago."

Maybe I *should* eat a little something, Charlotte thought. She was hungry after doing jetés all morning. The sandwich was sliced turkey with tomatoes and mayonnaise. It was very good.

"I remember when my mother signed me up for dance classes."

Charlotte looked up suspiciously. "Oh?"

"Not ballet classes—I had already had those—but ballroom-dancing lessons. As you know, I loved ballet. But ballroom dancing! Heavens! All us girls thought that was the *worst*."

Charlotte smiled, pausing for a moment in her chewing. Ballroom dancing would definitely be worse than ballet.

"And my best friend, Grace Hensler, did *not* have to take them. Her mother had resisted the pressure somehow. So I had to go alone."

Charlotte went back to her sandwich. She sensed a moral starting to creep into the story. "Let me guess," she said casually. "You started taking them, and found out that you loved ballroom dancing. You had a great time and made friends. Afterward you were glad your mother had made you."

"Actually, no, dear. What happened was that I had to get all dressed up twice a week to go to the Castle School of Dance and dance with those awful, gauche boys for an hour and a half. Every Tuesday and Friday. For six *months*."

"The boys were geeky?"

"They were terrible. Of course, they hated being there more than even we did, and they used to step on our toes on purpose, and pinch our backs, and make faces at us. Oh, those afternoons were such torture."

"Really?"

"Really. And I was shy, terribly shy, painfully shy. Some days I was so nervous about going that I almost—well—almost was sick to my stomach."

Charlotte stared at Nana. This was great. She never got to hear stories like this, about awful times from her parents' or grandparents' lives. She heard only about the happy stuff.

"What did you do?" she asked. She tried to imagine Nana very young, dressed in a frilly party dress, trying not to throw up.

"Well, I persevered. Not because of any strength of character, mind you, but because my mother would have killed me if I'd quit. After a while I made a few friends in that class—some of us girls banded together against those dreadful boys— and then toward the end, we convinced Mr. Dalrymple to teach us how to jitterbug. That was a lot of fun."

Charlotte nodded. "Nana, were you trying to get at something with this story?" Better to be direct.

"I think I was to begin with, but maybe the story didn't go exactly the way I intended it to," Nana admitted. "I guess what I really wanted to say is that maybe you're unhappy about this ballet class now, but it could be a lot worse, and anyway, it will be over soon enough." Nana paused, then she looked up and smiled at Charlotte. "And you're bound to get something out of it—ballet is truly a beautiful art. There—does that sound like how the story was supposed to turn out?"

Charlotte couldn't help laughing. "Yeah, that sounds more like it."

After lunch she went to her room, picked up Spike, and lay down with him on her chest. It made her feel better. So did Nana's ballroom-dancing story. Still, Charlotte knew that this recital was going to be the worst thing that ever happened to her.

7

The Backup Swan

The next day Charlotte and her classmates were officially told about their recital. They were indeed doing a short scene from *Swan Lake*. Louisa Ridley was to be the head swan. A few others were villagers. One of the boys was the head swan's boyfriend. The rest of the girls were backup swans. The recital would be on the last day of class, and all the other classes were giving performances that day too. Parents and friends were invited.

"As if I want any of my friends seeing me do that," Cathy whispered to Charlotte.

Charlotte nodded. "No joke," she whispered back.

Now, in addition to their usual warmups and practicing of the five basic positions, they learned a few more complicated movements. At the end of the week Madame Fisher began to separate the class into smaller groups to teach them their recital routines.

By the end of the fourth week, whenever the music to *Swan Lake* started, Charlotte's stomach automatically clenched, sweat broke out on her forehead, and she felt dizzy.

"Charlotte, dear, once more. Remember, it's two brief paces, then a lovely little arabesque, just so, then a delicate turn to the right, and . . ." Madame Fisher demonstrated the choreography again, humming along with the music under her breath.

Charlotte was embarrassed that she kept making mistakes. Cathy had already gotten the steps down. Charlotte could either keep time with the other students and not do the steps correctly, or she could do the steps correctly but completely out of pace with everyone else. She could not do both at once.

* * *

On the Monday before the Friday recital, Charlotte was at Cathy's house after class. They had eaten lunch and cheered themselves up by playing Leaves of Grass's latest CD.

"You have a neat room," Charlotte said, looking around. Cathy had big horse posters all over her walls. Her bookcase was filled with horse books like *Misty of Chincoteague* and *A Horse Called Wonder*. One shelf had a bunch of model horses on it, all lined up. Some of them were wearing little saddles.

"Thanks," Cathy said. "I hope you've noticed how there isn't anything with ballet on it in here."

Charlotte laughed. "Yeah, I noticed. But Cathy, you're actually pretty good in class—if Louisa the Please-a wasn't there, you'd almost be the best one. I have an excuse for hating it—I'm awful at it. But you're not."

Cathy shrugged. "I've been doing it a lot longer. That doesn't mean I like it. I just try to get through it. And anyway, even though they won't let me go to horse camp, at least I go to my uncle's farm in Mississippi for two weeks every summer.

He has horses, and I get to ride them. That's my favorite." She pointed to a large framed photograph of herself hugging a horse's head. "His name is Stardust. I'm going there a couple of days after the recital."

"Lucky you," Charlotte said enviously.

"In the meantime," Cathy said, jumping up and putting on a new CD, "we have work to do!"

The first lilting strains of *Swan Lake* filled the room, and Charlotte screamed and fell writhing to the floor.

Charlotte slept over at Annabel's house the next night. After dinner they watched *Return of the Body Snatchers* with Michael. Annabel's pet green snake, Wilfred, was snoozing on Annabel's shoulder. He seemed not to mind the scary parts.

After the movie was over, the girls went to Annabel's room and put Wilfred to bed in his aquarium, then got ready for bed themselves.

"So I think I have my routine down," Annabel said, pulling her curtains closed.

"I can't wait to see it," Charlotte said. She had already bought tickets to the day camp's fair for

her and her parents. Nana would already be gone by then.

"I think it's going to be fun," Annabel agreed. "We have neat costumes for our group floor routine. We're going to tie-dye T-shirts in arts and crafts. Then we'll paint our faces, you know, with rainbows and stars and flowers. I'm going to wear a headband, too."

Charlotte got out her brush. "So you'll be like flower children, huh? That'll be neat." She started working the brush through her blond tangles.

"Yeah," Annabel said. "I'm going to weave some flowers through my hair, too. We'll just sort of be generic hippies."

Charlotte nodded. "I know what you mean. I'm a generic swan," she said, and they both laughed.

Soon they were in bed with the lights out.

"Annabel," Charlotte said seriously, watching the moonlight make shadows on the walls, "I just don't think I can do it. I mean, I really don't think I can do it." She was near tears.

Annabel was silent for a minute. "What would happen if you said you were sick on the day of the recital?" Charlotte knew she meant, *How bad would it be?*

"Oh, I couldn't," Charlotte said with a sigh. "They would never go for it. I'd have to actually have chicken pox or something. I don't know what I'm going to do. I don't think I'll ever forgive my mom for doing this to me." She started crying then, trying to be quiet so Annabel's mom wouldn't hear.

Annabel patted her shoulder for a minute, then went to get the box of Kleenex from her desk. After she gave Charlotte a tissue, she went down the hall and got a glass of juice.

"Thanks," Charlotte whispered, taking the juice. They sat up in Annabel's bed in the dark, Charlotte sipping the juice and snuffling.

"I think you might just have to get through as best you can, then somehow forget it ever happened," Annabel said sympathetically. "Just tell yourself you'll never have to see those people again, and—"

"Except for Cathy Soames and Louisa Ridley," Charlotte reminded her.

"Yeah, but Cathy's nice and won't care if you mess up, and who cares what Louisa thinks? She's a nobody," Annabel said.

"What if she tells people at school? What if I run into people's parents at the grocery store, and they look at me and think, There's that loser who couldn't even handle being a backup swan?" Charlotte started crying all over again.

Annabel gritted her teeth. Charlotte knew that Annabel understood how she felt. They were helpless—there really wasn't anything either of them could do, and they knew it.

On Thursday Charlotte's mother asked her to say grace at dinner.

Charlotte sighed, closed her eyes, and put her hands together. Suddenly she realized that it was the only time she was allowed to have her elbows on the table, and she wondered why that was so.

"Charlotte?" her mother prompted.

"Dear Lord," Charlotte said. "Thank you for the gifts we are about to receive." If you can call liver a gift, she couldn't help thinking. "Thank you for letting us all be here together." Even though I will never forgive my mother for ruining my life. "Thank you that there's only one more day of ballet class, and after that it will be over forever and ever and I'll never have to do it again as long as I live," Charlotte said. She could hear her mother shifting in her chair. "And please, Lord, please don't let me make a complete and utter fool of myself tomorrow in front of everyone. Please let me get through it somehow and not totally embarrass myself in front of my parents and my grandmother. Amen." That ought to do it, she thought, opening her eyes and starting to eat.

8

A Graceful Swanlike Heap

Friday came. It was a horribly sunny day, clear and bright. Charlotte dragged herself into the kitchen, where her parents were already reading the paper. There were some Pop Tarts on a plate by the toaster, and Charlotte dropped them in the slots. She knew they were a peace offering—she was hardly ever allowed to have them. But she also knew that it would take more than Pop Tarts to make up for this.

The ballet academy's recital was taking place at a local high school, where there was a small auditorium and a stage. Charlotte's performance wasn't until eleven o'clock, but she had to be there at nine in order to get ready and watch the other classes perform. Annabel had asked if she'd like her to skip day camp in order to come, but Charlotte had insisted that she not do it.

"Believe me, Annabel. The last thing I want is for you to have a permanent memory of me in a pink tutu."

At nine Charlotte and her parents went to the high school. They all sat together in the audience and watched the very youngest classes do short group routines set to classical music. Charlotte was cheered by the way some of the younger kids made mistakes. One little girl who was around four years old simply wandered out of formation and came to sit on the edge of the stage. She waved at her parents and bounced her legs against the side. Her parents were videotaping the whole scene. They were chuckling.

Still, Charlotte knew that it was one thing for a four-year-old to mess up and another thing completely for someone who was almost eleven. Her mother put her arm across the back of Charlotte's chair and kept patting her shoulder. Charlotte ignored her.

As a bribe, her parents had offered to go out for

a nice lunch after the recital—Charlotte could choose where to go.

"How about Christian's?" Nana had suggested that morning. "That's a lovely place."

Charlotte remembered Christian's as being kind of dark inside, with white tablecloths and long benches covered in maroon leather. It was really for grown-ups.

"How about Père Antoine's?" Charlotte's mother had suggested. It was mostly an ice-cream parlor, although they had hamburgers, too. It was a fun place, with fabulous things to eat and loud music playing and toys hanging from the ceiling. Whenever they went there, Charlotte's father bet her a dollar that she couldn't eat a whole banana split all by herself. So far, she hadn't won, but she was working on it.

"Père Antoine's sounds okay," she said grudgingly.

Nana bit her lip. "But that's just an ice-cream parlor," she said. "Maybe we could go there for dessert. But don't you want to go to a nicer place for a real grown-up lunch with your parents and me?"

"Well, not really," Charlotte said truthfully.

"Aileen," Nana said softly, "how is she going to learn how to behave in certain settings if she's never called upon to do it? I remember when you were a child, I could take you anywhere and be sure that your manners were up to par."

"Now, now," Charlotte's father said. "We told Charlotte she could choose, and I think she's chosen Père Antoine's. Right, honey?"

Charlotte nodded. She could see Nana looking at her mother. Her mother's lips tightened.

"Why, I think Charlotte's manners are fine, Mother. This is her day, and we said she could choose." She looked down at Charlotte and smiled. Charlotte almost smiled back. "Père Antoine's it is."

Charlotte left then to get her costume, but she heard Nana starting up again.

"Aileen, don't you think that sometimes—"

"Mother, please give it a rest," Mrs. Hastings snapped. Charlotte paused on the stairs, her eyes wide. She had never heard her mother speak that way to Nana. On the other hand, Nana had been asking for it.

Now they were all sitting together in the auditorium. Charlotte's father was the only one who didn't seem tense and unhappy. Nana sat on the other side of Charlotte, holding her purse tightly in her lap. She and Charlotte's mother weren't speaking to each other.

After the youngest class, the second-youngest class performed a clown dance. Charlotte thought their costumes were kind of cute: they were all dressed as harlequins, and their dance seemed to be loosely choreographed leaping and jumping and running around. At ten thirty Charlotte left her parents and went backstage to change into her costume and start her warmup exercises.

Her class was in one of the small stuffy rooms beneath the stage. Overhead they could hear thumping and feet running. Charlotte and Cathy stood next to each other and got into their pink tutus. They were pale pink leotards on top but had stiff, frilly ruffles, made out of many layers of white and pale pink netting, sewn on the bottom.

Charlotte looked at herself in the brightly lit makeup mirrors. "I look like a chunky pink duck," she said sadly.

"I feel like one of those dancing mushrooms from that Disney movie," Cathy agreed.

"Girls! And boys," Madame Fisher added, clapping her hands. "It's time to prepare your makeup, then Miss Adelaide will lead you in your warmup exercises."

Some of the parents had volunteered to help backstage, and now they went around and put black eyeliner, blush, and lip gloss on each dancer. (Charlotte hadn't told her mother that she could volunteer if she wanted to.) Then everybody got a thick dusting of transparent powder. Charlotte wouldn't have minded the makeup if she hadn't known that shortly afterward she would have to go onstage.

Still, although she felt nervous and miserable, she didn't feel quite as bad as she had the night she'd slept over at Annabel's. She and Cathy had practiced their routine a lot on their own, and she felt she had finally memorized the steps in time to the music. Cathy had given her the tip that once onstage, whatever she did, she shouldn't ever look anywhere but at the dancer right in front of her.

"Why not?" Charlotte had asked.

"Just don't," Cathy replied tersely.

Miss Adelaide led the class in their warmups, and then all of a sudden it was time to go on. The girls (and the two boys) crowded into the wings of the stage, not talking, not daring to breathe. Cathy and Charlotte clutched each other's hands tightly in silent support. For a moment, Charlotte almost wished that Annabel was in the audience.

The music started, and Charlotte felt her stomach knot up. Her forehead was beaded with sweat, and she wondered what it was doing to her makeup. Then it was time, and all her thoughts stopped as she and the other secondary swans surged out onstage. Step, glissade, arabesque. Step, glissade, glissade, pirouette, dip, two quick steps. Charlotte had no idea how she was moving at all—she felt frozen, weird—as though she were in a movie. But she kept her eyes glued on Cathy's back in front of her and tried not to think, tried just to move to the music along with the others.

Their first little section was over, and the backup swans gathered in a circle and watched as Louisa performed her solo. As far as Charlotte could tell, it was perfect, just the way Madame Fisher had wanted. She let her gaze wander over to the wing, where Madame Fisher was standing watching them, her hands clasped in front of her.

"Go!" someone hissed in back of her. Charlotte started, then realized in panic that Cathy had already taken off and had joined the others in the second part of their routine.

Charlotte took several quick steps to catch up. In those horrifying instants, everything seemed to slow down so that she could see it all clearly in nauseating detail. She took rushed forward and accidentally bumped into Cathy, knocking her off balance a little. Cathy giggled, but managed to get herself back in line.

But Charlotte was thrown by Cathy laughing, and swung around too hard to the other side, where she bumped into Dawn Harris. Dawn didn't giggle. But now Charlotte knew that the audience must be aware that she was messing up. A picture of Nana at ballroom-dancing class, trying not to throw up, suddenly came to her.

She tried hard to concentrate on getting herself in line with the others and performed each of the movements as precisely as she could. But when she leaped up, everyone else was hitting the floor. When she swooped down in a swanlike movement, everyone else was pirouetting with their arms above their heads.

Through the buzzing sound in her ears, she thought she could hear the audience start to snicker. Out of the corner of her eye she was aware of Madame Fisher watching in the wings. Her parents and Nana must be watching too. She bit her lip and blinked her eyes, trying not to cry. The worst, the very worst, was happening.

Her head suddenly felt light, and there seemed to be something wrong with her eyes as she followed Cathy around onstage, trying to match her movements.

Then Cathy was staring at her as though through a long black tunnel. It was freezing on-

stage, Charlotte thought absently. Freezing and also weirdly hot.

Soon even Cathy's face went black, and Charlotte sank down in a graceful swanlike heap in the middle of the stage, completely passed out.

9

Ballet Class Survivor

"Some people will do anything for attention," Annabel said cheerfully, coming into Charlotte's room after dinner that night. She held a small bouquet of yellow roses, Charlotte's favorite.

"Here. My dad grew these."

"Thank you," Charlotte said, smiling and holding them to her nose. "Umm, these are fab."

"Oh, aren't you a darling, Annabel. They're lovely," Nana said, coming into the room. "Shall I put them in a vase, Charlotte dear?"

"Thank you, Nana," Charlotte replied. When Nana had taken the roses and gone, Charlotte smirked at Annabel. "You're a darling, dear," she said.

"What can I say? I can't help it," Annabel said

airily, bouncing on the bed. "So, what did it feel like to faint? I've never done it."

"Pretty yucky." Charlotte made a face. "I felt queasy for hours afterward. We didn't even go to Père Antoine's. But my parents said we could go there this weekend. Maybe you could come."

"That'd be great. Your folks don't think you did it on purpose or anything, huh?"

"No. Mom said there's no way I could have turned my face such an interesting shade of green." Charlotte rolled her eyes.

Annabel patted her hand. "Well, so the worst happened," she said sympathetically.

"Yep," Charlotte acknowledged.

"Do you think you'll ever get over it?"

"Maybe when I'm . . . oh, I don't know. Thirty." They both laughed.

The next day Charlotte and her parents took Nana to the airport. Her mother and Nana had been on their best behavior. At the gate to Nana's flight, they hugged and kissed as though they hadn't had any arguments at all.

"Thank you for a wonderful visit, my dear," Nana said to Mrs. Hastings.

"We enjoyed it, Mother. Start planning on another trip here soon."

Only Charlotte could see her father kicking her mother gently on the ankle.

"And you, my little ballerina," Nana said, taking Charlotte's face between her hands.

"Please, Nana. Anything but that," Charlotte said.

Nana smiled and kissed her. "You tried, darling. That's the important part. You're a very special little girl, and very pretty, too." She frowned, looking down at Charlotte's head. "Sweetheart, do you have to wear that thing in your hair? Surely there are more attractive ones. . . ."

"Now, Mother, Charlotte's scrunchy is fine. Have a safe trip."

"Good-bye," Charlotte's father said cheerfully.

"Bye, Nana. I'll miss you," Charlotte said.

"Bye, darlings!" Nana said, waving good-bye one last time as she boarded her plane.

"Well," Charlotte's mother said.

"Well," Charlotte's father said.

"It's just the three of us again. Isn't that nice?" Charlotte's mother asked her.

Charlotte nodded. "Especially since I don't have to go to ballet class anymore." She smiled.

Mrs. Hastings rolled her eyes and leaned against her husband, who put his arm around her, laughing.

The next Saturday was the day-camp fair that Annabel was performing in. Charlotte and her parents arrived in plenty of time to walk around and look at everything before Annabel's show.

There were booths selling things that campers had made in arts and crafts all summer, and others serving different kinds of foods. Parents had donated the food. Charlotte noticed a booth where you could make your own T-shirt. There were also booths giving out information about the day camp. Charlotte took some brochures.

Then they sat in the bleachers around the basketball court to watch Annabel's floor routine. Music began and Annabel's class, all dressed in their hippie costumes, ran out and got into formation. It was a great show. Everyone did everything perfectly in line, and it was a combination of fun dance steps and some floor gymnastics. Both Charlotte and her parents were very impressed by how well Annabel did everything. It was almost like watching a stranger. Charlotte saw Annabel's parents sitting a few rows down and waved to them. They looked pleased too.

After the floor show each person had to do a solo routine. Charlotte liked the performances on the uneven bars the best. There was a girl in Annabel's class who seemed really professional and talented, and Charlotte gasped when the girl dismounted by letting go of the top bar, flying through the air, then doing a backflip to land on her feet on the mat.

There's that backflip again, Charlotte thought grimly. Still, the uneven bars looked like the most fun in the world.

Then it was Annabel's turn on the horse. Basically she had to run up, bounce off a springboard, then leap over the horse. Sort of like a giant leapfrog, Charlotte decided. Annabel performed a couple of different jumps, but Charlotte had to agree that it wasn't nearly as fun or interesting as the uneven bars or the trampoline.

After her turn Annabel ran over, breathless. She was still in her hippie costume. Her parents hugged her and kissed her, and Charlotte and her family congratulated her too.

"You were wonderful, Annabel dear," said Charlotte's mother. "And Charlotte tells me you don't even like the horse."

"No, not really," Annabel said, looking flushed and happy.

"Yet you managed to do well on it, even though it wasn't what you wanted to do," Mrs. Hastings said.

Annabel smiled at her. "Well, no, I didn't really want to do it. But at least it wasn't ballet!" she said cheerfully.

"Gosh, I'm hungry," said Charlotte's father. "How about we get something to eat? I saw some hot dogs over there. Coming, dear?" He and Mrs. Hastings smiled good-bye and wandered over to the hot-dog booth.

"Look, Char—they're letting people take turns on the trampoline. Want to try?"

"Yeah! See you later, Mr. and Mrs. Bentley," Charlotte said.

"Okay, hon. Annabel, meet us back here in an hour, all right?"

"Sure, Mom."

Annabel and Charlotte ran over and got into line by the trampoline. There were two teachers spotting people who were jumping, and they were cautioning them not to try anything too tricky. But they were helping kids learn how to turn somersaults and flips.

Charlotte watched them carefully. Annabel was right—it did look easy to do when you just watched other people. Finally it was her turn. She scrambled up onto the high trampoline and took a few practice bounces. It was much, much better than jumping on a bed. She felt as though she were almost flying. She took three high bounces and turned a forward somersault. It was easy. She looked down at Annabel waiting her turn and laughed.

"Fun, huh?" Annabel asked with a big grin.

"Uh-huh!" Charlotte said, bouncing some more. The two teachers helped her do a backflip. They each stood on one side and put their hands at her waist. Then she bounced, and when they said "Go!" she jumped higher and they flipped her backward. It was so much fun. They did it once more, then said it was time to let someone else have a turn.

"Can I try one more?" Charlotte asked.

"Okay."

Charlotte bounced once, twice, three times. Then before the spotters knew what she was going to do, she jumped up, tucked her knees under, and flipped backward! She didn't land very well—she realized she should have jumped higher.

"Charlotte!" Annabel screamed. "You did it! You did it!" She was jumping up and down. Charlotte smiled down at her, then noticed her parents standing next to Annabel, looking amazed and happy.

"That was lovely, sweetheart," her mother called.

Charlotte beamed at her. Then Annabel was scrambling up next to her on the trampoline.

"See, you don't really bend that much at the waist," Charlotte explained. "In ballet class they

showed that you really bend most at your hips. So when you jump, think about your hips bending and pulling you backward."

Annabel nodded. Charlotte stepped over to the edge of the trampoline, and the two spotters got into place. Annabel bounced until she was high enough, then the spotters helped her flip. She landed on her feet.

"I think I see what you mean," she said to Charlotte with a thoughtful look. "You really do it with your legs, and not your stomach."

Annabel went into the middle again and bounced until she was very high. Then she jumped up, tucked her knees under, and went backward. Halfway through the leap she unbent her legs, and it pulled her the rest of the way around. She made a perfect landing.

Then Charlotte and Annabel were hugging and jumping up and down and laughing and screaming. "We did it! We did it!" they yelled.

Later on they were walking around eating ice-cream cones and looking at the booths.

"I can't believe your ballet class actually helped

me do a backflip," Annabel said, licking around her cone to keep it neat.

"I can't either. It was almost worth the torture. Almost, but not quite," Charlotte said.

Annabel punched her lightly on the arm. "So what about next year? Do you think your parents will let you go to day camp?"

"I don't know. I really hope so."

Just then Charlotte's parents walked up. "Are you girls having a good time?" Mr. Hastings asked.

"Yeah! This is the best part of the whole summer," Annabel said.

"Oh, honey, I have a little present for you," Charlotte's mother told her.

Charlotte watched curiously as her mother pulled something out of a bag. Then she and Annabel looked at each other and laughed.

Her mother was holding up a pink camouflage-pattern T-shirt that said "Ballet Class Survivor" on it.

"Oh, Mom, it's perfect!" Charlotte said, giving her mother a hug. "Just perfect."